Dec 10, 1985

For Michael Quinn

Michael Mullgym

THE SIGN IN
MENDEL'S WINDOW

THE SIGN IN MENDEL'S WINDOW

Mildred Phillips

ILLUSTRATED BY

Margot Zemach

Macmillan Publishing Company
· NEW YORK ·

Collier Macmillan Publishers
· LONDON ·

Macmillan Publishing Company
866 Third Avenue, New York, N.Y. 10022
Collier Macmillan Canada, Inc.

Printed in the United States of America

10 9 8 7 6 5 4 3 2 1

Library of Congress Cataloging in Publication Data

Phillips, Mildred.
The sign in Mendel's window.

Summary: When a stranger comes to Kosnov and accuses
Mendel the butcher of stealing his money, the whole
town joins in to show the police who is really guilty.
1. Children's stories, American.   [1. Butchers—
Fiction.   2. City and town life—Fiction]   I. Zemach,
Margot, ill.   II. Title.
PZ7.P546Si   1985   [E]   85-5049
ISBN 0-02-774600-3

To my friend Niels

M.P.

They called Kosnov a town. It was like calling a puddle a pond, a leaf a bush, a branch a tree. The whole town of Kosnov was no more than a dozen old wooden buildings huddled close, each leaning on its neighbor for support, just as the people who lived and worked in them did.

So when Mendel the butcher put the sign in the front window of his shop, the whole town came out to ask: Had Mendel and Molly struck it rich? Had fortune come knocking on their door? Why was the butcher shop FOR RENT? Goodness, could Mendel or Molly be sick?

"So many questions," Mendel said. "If only questions were zloty! Then we wouldn't have to rent out *half* the butcher shop!"

It wasn't a sudden gust of wind from the north that swept Mendel's hat off his head. It was the sigh of relief from his dear friends in Kosnov. Mendel and Molly were not leaving, and only half the shop would be rented.

Roshana the wigmaker kissed Tempkin the candlemaker, who hugged Simka the shoemaker, who hugged Mendel's wife, Molly, who, brushing away a joyful tear from her cheek, whispered to Mendel, "If only kisses and hugs could fatten the calf and buy feed for the chickens."

Mendel smiled. "Then, again, there'd be no need to rent, and we wouldn't be getting these kisses and hugs."

The new wall dividing the butcher shop was made by
Molly from two old bed sheets sewn down the middle,
bleached white until they dazzled and starched so stiff they
stood straight up like a board. Tacked to the ceiling and
tacked to the floor, the wall was better than perfect, Mendel
said. It didn't even have to be painted.

For many weeks, the sign sat in the window. Then one day, late in the afternoon, a gentleman came into town and stopped in front of the butcher shop window. He was wearing a wide-brimmed black felt hat trimmed with fur and a fine cloth coat. Mendel went to the door.

"Mr. Butcher," said the stranger, tipping his hat, "you are looking at a very lucky man. After traveling so far, I was worried indeed that upon arriving I would find your shop already rented."

Not often, thought Mendel, did such an eloquent and prosperous-looking gentleman come to Kosnov. Mendel was impressed. "And who is to say which of us is the luckier, Mr....?"

"Tinker. Tinker is my name."

"Come in, Mr. Tinker. Put down your bag and rest your feet."

Tinker entered and sat down on a wooden stool. Stroking his thick, black beard, he spoke. "I heard by word of mouth from an old acquaintance of a distant cousin's uncle in the city—may he rest in peace—that in this charming town there was a place for rent, a quiet room just right for my kind of work."

"Which is?" asked Mendel.

"I'm a thinker, Mr. Butcher. Tinker the thinker, a simple man with simple needs. For a humble meal and a place where I can think, I will gladly pay a week's rent in advance."

"Come take a look," Mendel said, leading the way out to a side door that opened directly into the new space. He stepped aside, saying, "Judge for yourself."

Moments later, Tinker returned. "It's a deal," he said as he paid the rent. Delighted, Mendel shook the gentleman's hand and wished him good night.

Soon it would be dark, for the sun was about to set. If only Molly weren't spending the night in Glitnik with her cousin. Mendel felt that if he didn't share the news, he would burst. He decided to drop in on Simka.

"Come in, landlord," Simka said jokingly.

"Already you know?" asked Mendel.

"Why else would a stranger stop right in front of the sign in your window? And why else would you be looking so pleased? So sit, Mendel, and tell me all about your new tenant."

While Simka worked on a pair of boots, Mendel gave an exact account of the meeting. "Imagine, Simka, so splendidly dressed and yet so humble, asking for nothing more than a place to work. Surely some divine providence has sent this great man to Molly and me."

Simka looked up. "Be careful," he warned. "Though it has only five letters, 'great' is a very big word. . . . You'll stay for supper? Don't worry, there's plenty."

Mendel felt very good.

What a busy week it was for Molly and Mendel in the shop. And with so many neighbors coming to welcome him, Tinker had little time in the day to do his work. But not once did he complain.

"A better tenant we couldn't have asked for," said Molly that Friday.

Late that day, as every Friday before the Sabbath began, Mendel was in his shop doing the books. It was his habit to count his weekly earnings aloud, dropping the coins one by one into a small wooden box that he kept on the shelf. So as not to disturb Tinker, he began in a whisper: "Five groszy, ten groszy, fifty groszy, one zloty, one zloty twenty, one zloty forty, two zloty—"

"Mendel, my friend," called Tinker, "you don't have to whisper. I enjoy the sound of your voice."

So Mendel counted louder: "Forty zloty seventy-one, forty zloty seventy-two, forty zloty and seventy-three groszy. That does it!"

"Your voice is like music to my ears," said Tinker. "Just once more!"

Flattered, Mendel counted again, this time chanting in his finest tenor voice. Still humming, he closed the box and put it on the shelf.

"I am thinking," called Tinker, "that I will go to the city for the weekend. May I borrow your horse?"

"Go in good health," said Mendel. "I will see you on Monday."

"First thing," answered Tinker. "First thing."

Just after sunrise on Monday morning, as Mendel was taking a few deep knee-bends in front of the window, he saw that his horse was back from the city, tied to the front post. But what were two other horses doing beside it?

Mendel dressed and went downstairs to his shop. Waiting for him there were not only Tinker but two uniformed policemen from the city, as well.

"Arrest that man!" shouted Tinker. "He is the man who stole my money, and the proof lies in that wooden box on the shelf. And in that wooden box are exactly forty zloty and seventy-three groszy. Count it, gentlemen. If it be so, then without a doubt the money is mine!"

Stunned and speechless, Mendel stared at a small hole in the partition, two inches from the floor. Not big enough for a mouse to get through, the hole was ample for a rat to get an eyeful.

Molly, awakened by all the commotion, rushed downstairs still in her nightgown. "Am I dreaming a nightmare?" she cried out. "What are you up to?"

"Forty zloty and seventy-three groszy," answered a policeman as he counted the last coin. "This proves without a doubt that your husband is a thief."

Molly laughed. "Mendel a thief? My Mendel is so honest that he wouldn't steal another man's joke. Mendel, darling, what happened?"

Mendel told her. "It hurts in my heart to know that I was fooled by fancy manners."

Just then, Simka's face appeared at the window. Molly rushed to open the door.

"I was worried that Mendel should go barefoot," said Simka, peering inside, "so I brought him his shoes, as good as new."

"In jail it doesn't matter," cried Molly. "Come in, Simka, and say good-bye."

"Are you going somewhere?"

"Not me, Simka. Him!"

Poor Mendel. A pair of handcuffs had been slapped on his wrists. "Mr. Policemen," cried Simka, "I am a senior citizen of Kosnov, and I demand to know what is going on!"

As the story unfolded, Simka nodded. "I'm a little deaf in my left ear," he said, "but from what I just heard it is perfectly clear that *Tinker* is the scoundrel."

"And where is your proof?" shouted Tinker.

Simka smiled. He whispered to the policemen, and one of them quickly left the shop.

Outside a crowd had gathered, as had dark clouds overhead.
Simka paced the floor.

It felt like an hour, but it was only a matter of minutes
before the policeman returned with his report. "How you
knew about the money is a mystery," he said to Simka.
"And, just as you said, everyone I questioned up and down
the street also knew, exactly to the groszy, how much was in
the wooden box. How is this possible?"

"I have the answer," said Tinker abruptly. "If a man is a thief, then why not a braggart, too?"

"I am not a judge," said the policeman. "We will have to take this case to the city!"

"Hold it!" Molly yelled. She flung open the door and called to her neighbors, "Get me a potful of scalding hot water!"

When this was done, Molly dumped all the coins from the wooden box into the water. Had Molly gone mad? What was she making?

Molly chuckled. "Groszy soup. And while it is cooking, I have three questions for Mr. Tinker.

"First," she began, "if you were a painter, what would be on your hands?"

"Paint, of course," answered Tinker.

"Second question. If you were a potter, would there be paint on your hands?"

"The answer to your foolish question is no! There'd be clay on my hands."

"Now let's say that you were a butcher. A customer just paid for his chicken. You took the coins and maybe put them in your pocket. My question is, would the coins be covered with clay?"

Tinker snickered. "If I were a butcher, the coins would be covered with—"

He looked into the pot. Skimming the surface, coating the water was a pale thin layer of fat. It had risen from the coins that lay on the bottom.

"A little fat?" Molly asked.

"A little fat," muttered Tinker.

As the handcuffs closed around his wrists, Tinker turned to Simka. "How *did* everyone know how much money was in the box?"

"Simple," said Simka. "Only a stranger like you wouldn't know that when our Mendel sings in his finest tenor voice, not only can everyone hear him, but we all stop to listen."

Tinker shrugged, and with a deep sigh he said, "I think I made a few mistakes. The biggest was coming to a little town like Kosnov."

At that, the whole town cheered. Yes, the whole town. Did
you know that the town of Kosnov was so small that when
Roshana the wigmaker sneezed, Mishkin the tailor said
"God bless you"—though he lived a dozen doors away?